To Roxy and Riley – P.D.

Clarion Books
215 Park Avenue South, New York, New York 10003

Text copyright © 2012 by Margaret Mahy
Illustrations copyright © 2012 by Polly Dunbar
First published in the United Kingdom in 2012 by Frances Lincoln Limited.
First American edition, 2012.

Clarion Books is an imprint of Houghton Mifflin Harcourt Publishing Company.

www.hmhbooks.com

The illustrations were executed in watercolor and collage.
The text was set in Heatwave.

Library of Congress Cataloging-in-Publication Data is available.
ISBN 978-0-547-81988-4

Manufactured in China
FL 10 9 8 7 6 5 4 3 2 1
4500346137

The Man
from the Land of
FANDANGO

Margaret Mahy

Polly Dunbar

Clarion Books • Houghton Mifflin Harcourt
Boston   New York   2012

The man from the land of Fandango

Is coming to pay you a call.

With his tricolor jacket and polka-dot tie
And his calico trousers as blue as the sky

And his hat with a tassel and all.

And he bingles and bangles and bounces–

He's a bird! He's a bell! He's a ball!
The man from the land of Fandango
Is coming to pay you a call.

Oh, whenever they dance in Fandango,
The bears and the bison join in,

And baboons on bassoons make a musical sound,

And the kangaroos come with a hop and a bound.

And the dinosaurs join in the din.

And they tingle and tongle and tangle

Till tomorrow turns into today,

Then they stop for a break and a drink and a cake

In their friendly fandandical way.

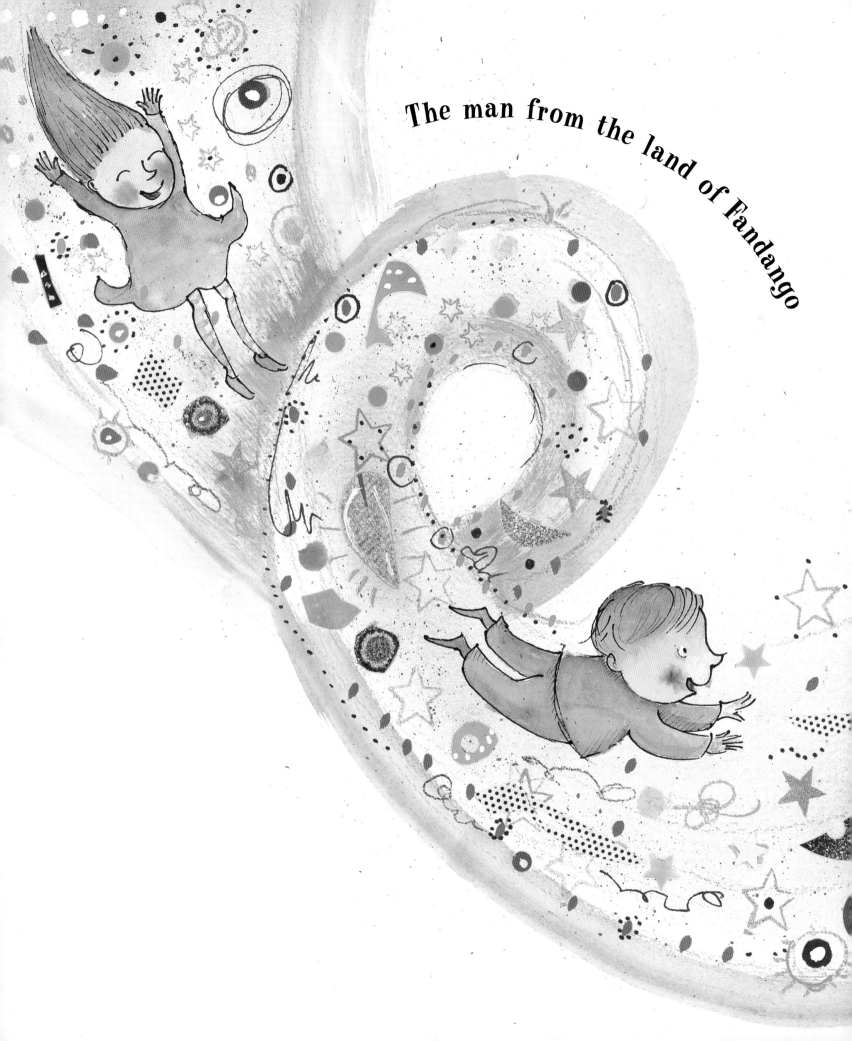

The man from the land of Fandango

Is given to dancing and dreams.

He comes in at the door like a somersault star

And he juggles with jelly and jam in a jar

And custards and caramel creams.

And he jingles and jongles and jangles

As he dances on ceilings and walls,

And he only appears every five hundred years—

So you'd better be home when he calls!